Pink Baby Alligator

Written by Judith A. Barrett
Illustrated by Emily D. Stewart

Printed in the United States of America.
Published by Marcinson Press, Jacksonville, Florida
© Copyright 2016 Judith A. Barrett & Emily D. Stewart

For bulk purchases or to carry this book in your
bookstore, library, school or other establishment,
please contact the publisher at marcinsonpress.com.

ISBN 978-0-9967207-5-5

Published by Marcinson Press
10950-60 San Jose Blvd., Suite 136
Jacksonville, FL 32223 USA
http://www.marcinsonpress.com

Find us on Facebook!
http://www.facebook.com/pinkbabyalligator

MARCINSON PRESS

Pink Baby Alligator

For Neela Ann Lisy

Reading is always a great idea!

Emily D Stewart

Written by Judith A. Barrett

ILLustrated by Emily D. Stewart

For beautiful, brilliant Hannah:
When you were four years old you asked
me to write down the pink baby alligator
story so you could read it yourself.
You always have great ideas! - JAB

For Aunt Joan, whose bedtime stories
inspired my imagination. - EDS

Once upon a time, there was a pink baby alligator who lived in the Florida Everglades. Her name was Rose.

Mama Alligator knew that Rose was going to be a special alligator even before she was hatched, because her egg's shell was a beautiful pink.

All the other baby alligators snapped and scratched at their eggshells. They were quickly hatched. But, baby Rose took a little longer and worked a little harder to get out of her shell.

When she was finally hatched and Mama Alligator saw how pink she was, Mama said, "This baby alligator's name is Rose. She knows how to figure things out and will have great ideas."

One day, Rose was sitting by herself, crying. Mama Alligator heard her and scurried to her baby. "What is wrong, Rose? Are you hurt?"

"No," Rose replied. "I was playing hide-and-go-seek with my sisters and brothers, but they always found me first. It isn't fun to play a game and always be the first one out."

Mama laughed. "Well, maybe hide-and-go-seek isn't your best game. It is easy to see you hiding in the green ferns or behind a palm leaf. You do stand out!"

"But Mama," Rose sobbed, "I don't want to stand out. I want to be like everybody else."

'POSSUM PAINT

Rose thought and thought.
She had a great idea! She went to the
'Possum Paint store and got green paint.

She painted her legs, feet, tail,
and face green. Rose worked very hard.
She even painted her back green.
Soon, Rose was green all over!

Rose ran out to play with her brothers and sisters. The baby alligators weren't playing hide-and-go-seek on the river bank anymore. They were playing hide-and-go-seek in the river and pretending to be logs.

Rose splashed into the water and pretended to be a log, too, but some of the paint washed off. Now she was green *and* pink. Rose was very sad. She was the first one out again.

Rose went for a walk by herself. She was feeling very lonely. As she walked along, she saw her friend, Petey Peacock.

"Petey, I am always the first one out when I play with my brothers and sisters because I stand out. Do you have any ideas for me?"

Petey said, "I fold up my beautiful tail when I don't want to stand out. Can you fold up your tail?"

"Not really," Rose replied, "but thank you."

Rose was even sadder as she walked down the path near the river. She looked up and saw her friend Carl Cardinal in a tree. Rose called up to him,

"Carl, I am always the first one out when I play with my brothers and sisters because I stand out. Do you have any ideas for me?"

Carl said, "I like to stand out. I flit from branch to branch so that other cardinals can see me. You could ask them to play a game where the winner is the one who stands out."

Rose didn't think her brothers and sisters would play a game like that, but she said "thank you" to Carl, because she was polite.

Rose couldn't imagine that she could be any sadder. She flopped down on a log and started crying great big alligator tears.

"Whoooooo is that crying?" a voice asked. Rose looked all around and couldn't see anyone. She began crying even harder.

"I said, whooooo is that crying?
And why are you crying?" Rose looked
up and she saw Oliver Owl blinking
at her.

"It's me, Rose, the pink baby alligator.
I'm crying because I am always
the first one out when I play
with my brothers and sisters,
because I stand out.
Oliver, do you have any
ideas for me?"

"Well," Oliver said, "if I were playing a game and didn't want to stand out, I would stand next to a brown tree. Then I wouldn't stand out. Have you tried standing next to a brown tree?"

Rose jumped up, ran around, and said,
"Thank you, Oliver! Thank you!
You just gave me a great idea!"

"You're quite welcome," said Oliver,
as he scratched his brown head, wondering
what the great idea was.

Rose hurried home. Her brothers and sisters were all there, getting ready to start another game of hide-and-go-seek.

"Oh, Rose," said her sister Allie, "are you sure you want to play? You always seem so sad when you are the first one out. Would you like to be referee and keep score instead?"

"It's okay," Rose said. "I have a plan!"

Allie was "It." First she found Alvin.
Then she found Gail, Alice, and Glenn.
She found Tory, Flory, Missy, and Jesse.
She found all the brother and sister
alligators – except for Rose.

All the brothers and sisters began helping Allie look for Rose. Even Petey Peacock, Carl Cardinal, and Oliver Owl joined in the hunt to look for Rose. "Rooooooose!" everyone called as they looked behind trees, in the lagoon, and under the ferns. But, no Rose!

Finally, Allie asked Filomena Flamingo,
"Fil, have you seen Rose?"

Filomena looked around and giggled.
All the flamingos giggled.

Then Allie heard, "Here I am!"
Allie looked closer, and there was Rose,
standing next to Filomena, in the middle
of all the beautiful pink flamingos.
Petey, Carl, Oliver, and all the brothers
and sisters laughed with Allie.

"Rose," said her brother Jesse,
"It was fun playing a game where
everyone was included!"

"Like Mama says, you
always have great ideas!"

Grown-ups!

If you and your child enjoyed this book, make your voice heard.

Want to see more of Rose and her friends? Would you like to see more books about diversity and inclusion?

You can make it happen!

We would greatly appreciate your taking a quick minute or two to write an online review for this book. Online reviews are an extremely important tool for readers, authors, libraries, schools, and bookstores to spread the word about interesting new books. Every review counts.

Thanks and happy reading!

Find Pink Baby Alligator and her friends online:
www.facebook.com/pinkbabyalligator

57147005R00022

Made in the USA
Lexington, KY
07 November 2016